For William and Emma xx – LR

For Ed, the bearded man in my life x – KH

First published in 2020 by Scholastic Children's Books
Euston House, 24 Eversholt Street
London NW1 1DB
a division of Scholastic Ltd
www.scholastic.co.uk
London – New York – Toronto – Sydney – Auckland
Mexico City – New Delhi – Hong Kong

PB ISBN 978 1407 19126 3
C&F PB ISBN 978 0702 30322 7

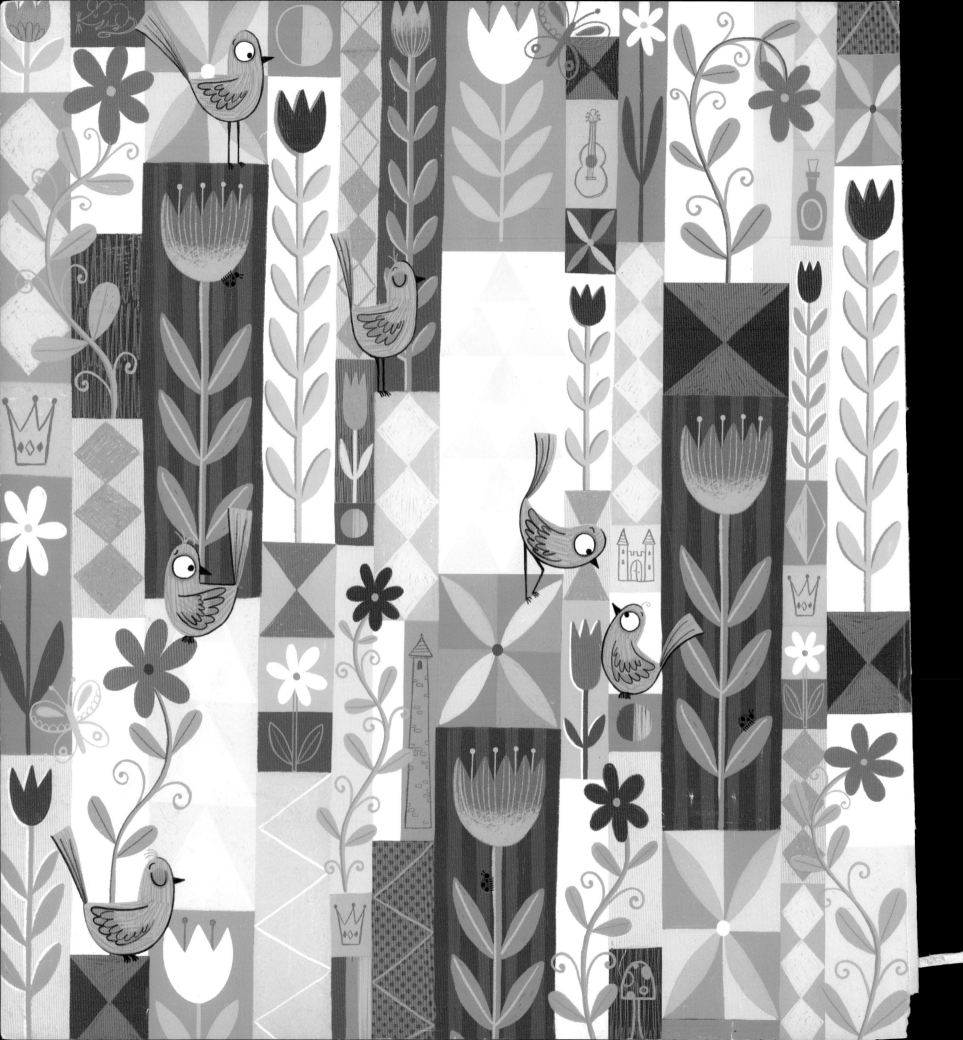

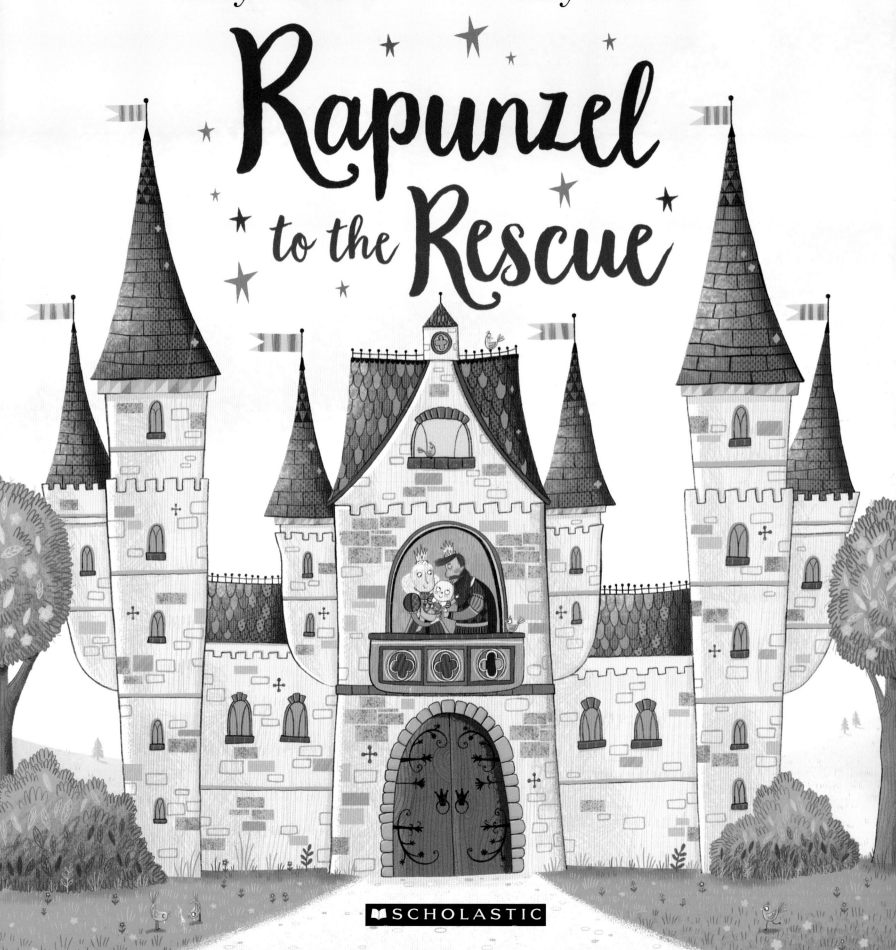

Lucy Rowland   Katy Halford

Rapunzel
to the Rescue

SCHOLASTIC

You might think this story is one that you know.
Rapunzel – the girl in the tower?

But no!

See, long long ago in the dead of the night,
a **witch** stole a baby, yes that bit was right.

But it **wasn't** a girl.
No, this bundle of joy . . .

was the King and Queen's **son,**
such a **sweet** little boy.

The witch knew the baby
had **hair** that could **heal**!

She cut off small strands
(which she ate with a meal!).

The hair kept her **strong**
and in **very** good health –

the prince soon had curls
which she sold for great wealth.

And as he grew older the witch, with a grin,
was pleased to see hair . . .

sprouting out
of his chin.

The witch knew this beard
had a **very** strong **power**,

so **locked** the prince up
in a rickety **tower**.

She visited daily to **snip** at his hair,

then off she would go again,
leaving him there.

The prince, through the years,
became **tall** and quite **strong**.

And his **beard** (what a beard!) grew **incredibly** long!

By now, you'll be thinking, Rapunzel?

Where's she?

Just look – in that forest glen, under the tree –

a girl singing songs
in a lovely soft voice.

LA LA LA LA LA LA

TOWER
CASTLE
RAPUNZEL'S HOUSE

She has to make money,
she hasn't a choice –

enough for some milk
and some cheese and some bread,

to help her poor mother
who's poorly in bed.

One morning, the prince in his room, feeling bored,
sprang straight to his feet when he heard a loud chord.

"That music!" he shouted out, spinning around,

"I've just never heard such a beautiful sound!"

He spied young Rapunzel
from high up above
and knew, in that moment . . .

he'd fallen in love.

Rapunzel came back again later that day,
she saw a strange lady, and watched in dismay
as something so hairy
began to unravel –

it whooshed
down the tower
and fell in the gravel!

And here's where our story
gets ever so weird –

That lady? She started to climb up the beard!

A few moments later
she clambered
back
down.

With bottles of hair,
she set off towards town.

Rapunzel thought
"Gosh!
What was happening there?!"

So slowly but surely she
climbed up the hair.

But reaching the window, she started to wince,
"This hair," blushed Rapunzel "belongs to a . . .

prince!"

The prince told his story, his head in his hands,
while clever Rapunzel sat dreaming up plans . . .

"It's simply **OUTRAGEOUS**. A terrible thing!

Someone should call up the
Queen and the King!

The witch cuts your hair and then sells it in town?
We'll teach her a lesson!" she said with a frown.

As planned, the next morning,
the young Prince appeared.
Rapunzel was ready
and climbed up his beard.

The witch, as expected,
turned up around ten,

"PRINCE! Throw down your beard!"

she shouted again.

and the witch held the silky beard up to her face.

But magical hair is a very strange thing . . .

it started to stick to

the mean witch's chin!

Back at the palace, the King and the Queen
arranged the best banquet there ever has been!

Rapunzel worked hard for the whole of the summer.
The prince (still in love) joined her band as a drummer.

He'd grown a new beard and his hair had been clipped.
The rest of the band were all **styled** and **snipped**.

And now people travel
from near and from far,

for the **Scary-Hair Band**
and Rapunzel's guitar.

YAY!

THE SCARY-HAIR BAND RULE!!!

RAPUNZEL WILL YOU MARRY ME?